CHOOSE YOU...

THE W...
AND THE UNICORN

BY DEBORAH LERME GOODMAN

ILLUSTRATED BY SUZANNE NUGENT
COVER ILLUSTRATED BY MARCO CANNELLA

CHOOSECO
WAITSFIELD, VERMONT

Book design: Stacey Boyd, Big Eyedea Visual Design
Book layout: Jamie Proctor-Brassard, Letter10 Creative

For information regarding permission, write to:

CHOOSECO
P.O. Box 46
Waitsfield, Vermont 05673
www.cyoa.com

Publisher's Cataloging-in-Publication Data

Names: Goodman, Deborah Lerme, author. | Nugent, Suzanne, illustrator.
| Cannella, Marco, illustrator.
Title: The warlock and the unicorn / Deborah Lerme Goodman. ;
illustrated by Suzanne Nugent ; cover illustrated by Marco Cannella..
Description: Waitsfield, VT : Chooseco, 2023. | 30 b&w illustrations.
| Series: Choose your own adventure. | Audience: Ages 9-12. | Summary:
In this interactive adventure book, a warlock casts a spell of eternal
winter over Flanders and the reader must find a silver unicorn to break
the curse.
Identifiers: ISBN 9781954232136 (softcover)
Subjects: LCSH: Magic -- Juvenile fiction. | Unicorns -- Juvenile
fiction. | Warlocks -- Juvenile fiction. | Flanders - Juvenile fiction.
| LCGFT: Plot-your-own stories. | BISAC: JUVENILE FICTION / Animals /
Dragons, Unicorns & Mythical. | JUVENILE FICTION / Fantasy & Magic. |
JUVENILE FICTION / Interactive Adventures.
Classification: LCC PZ7.1 G66 2023 | [FIC]--dc22

Published simultaneously in the United States and Canada

Printed in Canada

10 9 8 7 6 5 4 3 2 1

To my brave and big-hearted brother, Keith

BEWARE and WARNING!

This book is different from other books.

You and YOU ALONE are in charge of what happens in this story.

There are dangers, choices, adventures, and consequences. YOU must use all of your numerous talents and much of your enormous intelligence. The wrong decision could end in disaster—even death. But don't despair. At any time, YOU can go back and make another choice, alter the path of your story, and change its result.

Not long after you rescued your small Flemish village from a dangerous drought, the village is struck by another disaster: an evil warlock has cast a spell so that winter never ends. The only way he will reverse the unending snow and cold is if someone brings him a silver unicorn. The problem? No one has ever seen one. Do they even exist? You must decide: do you leave your village to battle the warlock on your own or do you go in search of a silver unicorn?

Even though it's early May, snow still blankets the ground in Flanders. By now, there should be green furrows in the soil, but the only furrows you see are on the anxious faces of your neighbors in the village. Sheep and cows should be grazing on fresh spring grass, but they desperately poke their noses at the snow, growing hungrier each day. Everyone is worried about running out of food before spring crops can be harvested. Everyone looks at you expectantly.

They know you can't control the weather, but they remember that just a year ago, in 1507, you saved the villagers by finding a unicorn to purify the water of their well. You need a unicorn again. However, this time, it has to be a silver unicorn, and who knows if that even exists?

The local warlock has decided he wants a silver unicorn and won't let winter end until he gets one. The villagers are used to the warlock's whims, so they don't question the fact that he thinks a silver unicorn would be a pretty thing to have. What the warlock wants, he usually gets. He reasons that if people aren't busy planting, they'll have time to search for a silver unicorn. What's more, if they're hungry, they'll have to go into the forest to scavenge for food, and they can just as easily keep an eye out for a silver unicorn. The only thing is, weeks have passed, and no one has even glimpsed a silver unicorn.

Turn to the next page.

2

You trudge through the snow to Marie-Claire's cottage. She's the oldest person in the village and your special friend. You know it's hard for her to get around in the snow, so you want to see if she needs any help. Also, maybe she'll offer you a bite to eat! Your empty stomach rumbles.

As Marie-Claire hands you a cup of hot water with some herbs floating on the surface, she says, "I'm sorry I can't offer you milk, but my cow isn't eating enough to give me any now. This unending winter . . ."

You see that she's fighting back tears. You understand immediately that Marie-Claire is wondering how much longer she can live unless spring comes.

Go on to the next page.

"I'm going to find the silver unicorn!" you announce with more confidence than you feel. "If anyone can find a unicorn, it's me!"

Marie-Claire pats your hand. "That's very brave of you," she says, "but I'm not sure it's a good idea. Even if you do find a silver unicorn and deliver it to the warlock, what next? He might allow us spring this year, but the next time he wants something, he knows that all he has to do is extend winter and we'll do whatever he says. The problem is not finding a silver unicorn; the problem is the warlock."

Turn to the next page.

4

You're silent for a while. You feel even less certain about managing the warlock than you do about finding a silver unicorn. "What am I supposed to do about the warlock?" you ask. "Even if I could defeat him—and I'm not sure I can—it doesn't make sense, because who would end winter for us if he's gone?"

"Oh no, you can't overpower the warlock," Marie-Claire quickly agrees. "I'm not sure that's even possible. Even though he is incredibly dangerous, you might be able to trick him or make some kind of a deal with him."

She lovingly touches your cheek. "I wish it didn't have to be you to take this kind of risk."

You look at her skeptically. "Anything involving the warlock sounds frightening. Maybe I should try to find the silver unicorn and let someone else handle the warlock."

"It's your decision. Everyone will be grateful no matter what you decide," says Marie-Claire, "but sooner or later, someone has to deal with the warlock."

If you decide to search for a silver unicorn, turn to page 6.

If you decide to deal directly with the warlock, turn to page 8.

6

"I'm good at finding unicorns," you say. "I'm going to look for one, and we can worry about the warlock after he puts an end to this winter. Now tell me, what do you know about silver unicorns?"

Marie-Claire shakes her head. "I'm not convinced such a thing exists. However, if silver unicorns do live in Flanders, don't you think the Duke might have one?"

"Maybe," you agree, "but if the Duke has a silver unicorn, why wouldn't he have offered it to the warlock already?"

"Who knows where the Duke is now? He's always traveling from one castle to another. It might not still be winter where he is."

Go on to the next page.

You wrap your hands around your cup, trying to warm them. "That's true, but if he's always traveling, how can I find him? I have another idea. I might be able to learn more about a silver unicorn from a regular unicorn."

"That's a thought, but it's not as if anyone has found a regular unicorn lately either," says Marie-Claire. "No matter what you decide, it won't be easy, and your chance of success is small. Which possibility excites you more?"

If you decide to see if the Duke has a silver unicorn, turn to page 10.

If you decide to get help from a regular unicorn, turn to page 12.

8

"You're right," you tell Marie-Claire. "I have to deal with the warlock directly. Maybe I can try to talk him out of this crazy desire for a silver unicorn. Maybe if he knew how much we were suffering . . ."

Marie-Claire shakes her head. "No, you're going to need magic, and much more magic than the little bit I can create. If I were you, I'd see if the sorceress can help you."

"Is her magic as powerful as the warlock's?" you ask.

"It's different magic. The sorceress is rarely evil, so if you can find her, she'll probably be willing to help you. Whether she can end the warlock's spell is hard to say. I know you managed to find the sorceress last year, but now that her location has been discovered, I doubt she's still there. Finding her again might be a challenge."

You remember all the trouble you went through to find the sorceress last year. "You're right. Finding the sorceress might not be any easier than finding a silver unicorn! Do you have any other ideas?" you ask.

"You could try to lure the warlock to the Stream of Lost Memories. Maybe if he steps in, he'll forget that he wanted a silver unicorn."

"The Stream of Lost Memories?" you exclaim. "What's that?"

"It's a place where people go to forget children and lovers they've lost."

You can't believe you're hearing about this for the first time. "How come I never knew about this before?"

Go on to the next page.

"There was no reason for you to know," says Marie-Claire. "You've never been sad enough."

You stand up indignantly. "My parents died! I think I know what sadness is!"

Marie-Claire takes your hand consolingly. "No, with you it was different. It's important that you remember *everything* about your parents. They wouldn't have wanted you to forget them. This is for people with hopeless, broken hearts."

As you choke back tears, you notice the icicles formed by leaks in Marie-Claire's roof. One more snowstorm and her roof might collapse!

"Tell me what happens with this stream. People wade in and they forget everything?"

Marie-Claire shivers. "It's risky. You can never be sure exactly which memory will be washed away. Sometimes people have to go in several times before they forget the memory that pains them. You probably won't get more than one chance with the warlock."

"That sounds dangerous. Maybe it's better to look for the sorceress, although it was pretty hard to find her last year," you say.

"None of this is going to be easy," Marie-Claire tells you. "But no one else seems to be doing anything about the fact that we are going to starve if spring doesn't arrive very soon."

If you decide to get help from the sorceress, turn to page 14.

If you decide to lure the warlock to the Stream of Lost Memories, turn to page 17.

"I'm going to see if the Duke has a silver unicorn!" you announce.

Marie-Claire blows on her freezing hands, and you realize your own fingers are numb with cold too.

"If he has a silver unicorn, are you going to beg him to let you have it or try to steal it?" she asks.

As usual, Marie-Claire is one step ahead of you!

"If I beg the Duke for a silver unicorn, do you think he'd give it up?"

Marie-Claire pauses to think. "Of course, I've never met him, so I really can't say what kind of person he is. What I do feel certain about is that the Duke is not suffering as much as we are. He surely has reserves of food and plenty of firewood. A silver unicorn must be very valuable, so he won't hand it over without a lot of persuasion." She smiles at you warmly. "I must say, you are very good at persuasion. It's possible the Duke would listen to you."

Go on to the next page.

"You're right that no one would be quick to give up a silver unicorn," you reply. "It might be easier to just steal it."

"A silver unicorn is not something you can just sneak into your pocket," Marie-Claire points out.

"No, but I could ride the unicorn away."

Marie-Claire sighs. "Without anyone seeing you? Everyone has an eye out for a silver unicorn. How do you think you can ride away unnoticed?"

"At night?" you suggest.

"Anything involving the Duke is going to be tricky," says Marie-Claire. "Whether you choose to beg for a silver unicorn or just steal one, you'll need to be very clever."

*If you decide to beg for the silver unicorn,
turn to page 20.*

*If you decide to steal it,
turn to page 24.*

"I'm going to look for a regular unicorn," you announce. "First of all, it may lead me to a silver unicorn, and if it doesn't, maybe we can figure out a way to turn it silver."

Marie-Claire nods her head. "Yes, that's not a bad idea. People say the sorceress has some spells of silver. If you do find a unicorn, she might be able to turn it silver." She stands and wraps a scarf around you. "Don't get too cold."

When you begin stomping through the snowy forest, there's no way to avoid being cold. Your nose and fingertips feel like needles of ice are pricking them. However, walking in the snow takes a lot of effort. By the time you reach the birch grove, you hardly feel the cold at all.

You pause to admire the sunlight glistening on each ice-coated branch. You watch squirrels chasing each other from one tree to another, but then you hear a whimpering sound.

As you look around for where the cries are coming from, you hear another sound—the flapping of many wings. You turn your face to the sky in time to see a dozen silvery birds fly overhead. You've never seen birds like this, and you wonder where they're going. Could there be a silver unicorn where silver birds nest?

You are just about to follow the flying birds when you again hear the heartbreaking cries of an animal in pain. Can you ignore this suffering to follow the silver birds?

Go on to the next page to make your choice.

If you decide to find the creature that is crying,
turn to page 36.

If you decide to follow the silver birds,
turn to page 44.

14

"If I'm going to need magic," you say, "the sorceress is my best bet. Do you think I should at least look where I found her last year?"

Marie-Claire shrugs. "With the sorceress, you never know. You may as well start there. Good luck, and give her my regards!"

Last year, the sorceress was living in the hills outside the village. You can't skate there, so it's a long, slow slog through the snow. Unfortunately, when everything is covered with snow, it's hard to tell one hill from another. You are soon cold and exhausted.

You pause to catch your breath. The woods seem strangely quiet. There's no chatter of squirrels or chirps of birds. Suddenly, a lavender tornado slowly whirls past you, winding between the trees. You remember the sorceress telling you that she did her best thinking when she was disguised as wind, so this must be her! But how to get her attention? You have to act quickly!

If you call out to her, will she hear you when she's the wind? Maybe you should just throw yourself into the tornado to make her stop.

*If you call out to the swirling lavender mist,
turn to page 29.*

*If you hurl yourself into the purple tornado,
turn to page 93.*

"Tell me how to find the Stream of Lost Memories," you say.

You listen intently as Marie-Claire describes its location. "You'll have to lure the warlock there," she says. "It's going to be a long walk from where the warlock has been spending the winter, and you'd better be careful he doesn't try anything devilish along the way."

You shudder at the thought of spending so much time with the warlock.

"I'll be careful," you reply.

Marie-Claire hugs you goodbye. You hope she'll be all right while you're away.

In winter, the fastest and easiest way to travel is along the frozen river. You stop at your own cottage to get your skates. At the riverbank, you strap your skates on, then step onto the ice. You wave to your neighbors. Some are fishing from holes cut in the ice, and younger kids are skating around playing tag. You don't tell them where you're going.

When you reach the windmill, you climb onto the snowy riverbank and remove your skates. You wedge them between some large rocks and pile a little snow on top to hide them. Then you start trudging through the snow to where the warlock is rumored to spend the winter.

You come to a man sitting on a stone wall. You are about to ask if he's seen the warlock when you notice he's eating a bird. You gasp with horror as feathers flutter from his mouth. He looks up at you with his red eyes, and you know you've found the warlock.

Turn to the next page.

You try to hide your revulsion and say cheerfully, "I've found a silver unicorn for you!"

The warlock finishes crunching some bones and wipes a feather off his lip. "Where is it?"

"It's a few hours away from here," you reply, and suddenly you think again about just how awful that time with him will be.

"Go get it," the warlock orders. He picks up some feathers from his lap and pops them in his mouth.

"I tried," you say, "but this silver unicorn is really large. It's much bigger than any regular unicorn, and look at me. I'm a kid. I need your help to get it."

The warlock smiles eagerly. "Just how big is it?"

"Quite a bit bigger than any horse I've ever seen!"

"All right," says the warlock eagerly. "Take me there."

You lead the warlock through the forest. Having him walk behind you makes you very nervous, so you glance back at him from time to time. His red eyes are riveted on you.

Trudging through the snowy forest is exhausting. Your nose, ears, and fingers are freezing, but the rest of you is sweating with exertion. You hear the warlock make strange snorting sounds, and quickly look back to see if he's getting ready to do something evil.

Go on to the next page.

"What's that sound?" you ask. "Were you making magic?"

The warlock laughs. "How little you know about magic! If I were casting a spell, I'd make sure you didn't hear it!"

That makes you even more nervous! You decide to make conversation to distract him from getting any devilish ideas.

"Do you know how much everyone is suffering because of this unending winter?" you ask him.

The warlock snickers. "How would I know?"

Just then it occurs to you that maybe he really *doesn't* know the misery he's caused. You could make him understand, but how?

Maybe you could tell him a story to explain how hard it's been. You could exaggerate a little and put in some dramatic twists to get your point across. Or maybe you could just bring him to your village so he could see for himself. If he saw how difficult life was there, maybe he would end winter, but how will your neighbors feel about the warlock showing up? Maybe it's best just to continue on to the Stream of Lost Memories, even though it's still hours away.

If you decide to tell him a story of winter suffering, turn to page 33.

If you invite him to your village, turn to page 46.

If you decide to continue on to the Stream of Lost Memories, turn to page 75.

"I'm going to tell the Duke how desperate we are, how badly we need a silver unicorn. I'm going to beg!" you tell Marie-Claire.

"People say he's not unkind," she replies. "I hope he listens to you!"

In winter, the fastest route to the Duke's castle is the frozen river, so you get your skates and head to the shore. Half the village seems to be on the ice already. Because nothing can grow, many of your neighbors have cut holes in the ice and are fishing. You carefully skate around them.

Skating is your favorite thing about winter. As you glide toward the castle, you almost forget your empty stomach. You extend your arms and imagine you are flying along the ice!

You've never been to the Duke's castle before, and it's farther than you had expected. When you finally reach it, you discover it's also much larger than you had expected. You hide your skates in the bushes by the riverbank and approach the guards standing by the entrance of the castle walls.

"I'd like to speak to the Duke, please," you tell them. "He needs to know how this unending winter is causing the villagers to starve. The warlock wants a silver unicorn, and if the Duke has one, he really should give it to the warlock so we can all have spring."

The guards smile at you with amusement.

"As it happens," one guard replies, "the Duke is well aware of the problem. He's not here now because he's gone to find a silver unicorn."

"Oh, that's wonderful news!" you exclaim.

Turn to page 22.

The other guard says, "I'm not so sure it is. The Duke has been gone for a month already. If it were easy to get a silver unicorn, he'd be back by now."

"Oh." At that moment, you decide you'll search for a silver unicorn too, on your own. You know your neighbors have searched the forest near your village, but maybe there's one hiding in the forest here.

You say goodbye to the guards and enter the woods beside the castle walls. There's no path, so walking through the snow is slow and awkward. Your boots are wet, and your feet are cold. Your teeth start to chatter.

Go on to the next page.

There's flash of red between the trees and a fox appears. You stop to look at it. The fox fearlessly gazes back at you.

You know foxes can be very tricky, but you've never heard of them attacking a person. Still, there's no one else around, and you don't have any way to defend yourself. Your heart starts to pound.

The fox barks at you, and for some reason it sounds like the word "Why."

"I'm looking for a silver unicorn," you reply.

The fox barks again and chases its tail in a circle. When it barks a third time, it sounds like "Come!"

"Come with you?" you ask. "You know where there's a silver unicorn?"

The fox barks once more and takes a small leap into the air.

You hesitate. Everyone knows that foxes are tricksters. Also, is this fox even speaking or are you desperate enough to imagine its barks are words? Yet, you remind yourself that you have no other clues and are really just wandering in the forest, hoping to find a silver unicorn. Maybe you should follow the fox.

If you decide to turn away from the fox, turn to page 49.

If you step toward the fox, turn to page 71.

"I'm going to steal the Duke's silver unicorn—if he has one," you reply. "I think I'd better have help for that, so I'm going to ask Wiets to come with me."

Marie-Claire raises one eyebrow. "That boy is nothing but trouble, so he should be good at stealing."

"Marie-Claire! Wiets is my best friend!" you exclaim. "But you're right. He *is* good at stealing!"

You say goodbye to Marie-Claire and return to your own cottage to grab your skates. With the river frozen and the roads icy with packed snow, skating along the river will be the fastest way to the Duke's castle.

On the way to the river, you stop by Wiets's cottage. You find him shoveling a clearing for his three cats. As soon as you ask him to join you in stealing a silver unicorn, he drops his shovel and shouts, "Yes! Let me get my skates!"

A few minutes later, the two of you are gliding along the river. The cold air reddens your cheeks, but the rest of you warms up quickly. Lots of other villagers are on the frozen river too. Some have cut holes in the ice and are fishing. Others are pulling small sleds toward neighboring villages, maybe sharing food or hoping to barter for some. Small kids are just sliding around on their bottoms. You grin at Wiets and challenge him to a race.

You skate farther than you've ever gone before, until you see the high walls of a castle rising on the riverbank. Even though you've heard about the Duke's castle, this is the first time you're seeing it, and the size makes you skid to a stop.

Go on to the next page.

"This is bigger than our church!" you exclaim.

"It's the biggest building I've ever seen," Wiets agrees. "I don't know how we're going to sneak in."

You take his hand and say, "Let's investigate!" The two of you hide your skates in some bushes, then head up a path toward the entrance. You're so excited that you break into a lighthearted skip, and that makes you stumble in the snow. As you regain your balance, you see the two guards posted on either side of an opening in the massive wall surrounding the castle.

"We could say we're new servants," you suggest to Wiets.

"That's a great idea," says Wiets. "Let's go!"

You politely introduce yourselves to the two guards as new servants. They must not think you look suspicious, because they wave you into a courtyard without a single question.

This place is bustling with activity! Steam rises from the laundry that servants are scrubbing. Other servants are chopping wood. Children are playing with balls and hoops. No one looks hungry.

You and Wiets eye each other with excitement. You take each other's hand and proceed into the castle. Your footsteps echo in the grand hall. Unlike in the courtyard, there's no one there, so you take your time to admire the paintings of finely dressed people that line the corridor. You run your hand along elaborately carved trunks.

Turn to page 27.

Then something shiny catches your eye. It's a display cabinet full of silver animals, each the size of a robin. You gaze in awe at the metal menagerie. There's a silver horse, a fox, a pheasant, a strange animal with huge ears and a snake-like nose, and . . . a unicorn!

Wiets grins at you mischievously. You know what he's thinking.

"No, don't," you warn, and step away from the cabinet of silver statues. You move behind a giant shield.

Wiets snatches the silver unicorn and tucks it into his pocket! He turns to you victoriously.

Suddenly, a servant pins Wiets to the wall and shouts, "Thief! Thief!"

Where did this person even come from? you wonder. You crouch behind the shield as more servants scurry over. A guard smacks Wiets across the face, then rummages through his pockets.

"You're off to the dungeon until the Duke can decide what to do with you!" another guard announces. He grabs Wiets by the arm and starts to drag him away.

An elegant woman draped in velvet and furs strides up, and the crowd of servants parts. "He's just a boy," she says. "Look how thin he is."

Wiets is trembling with fear. His face is turned to the ground.

Turn to the next page.

"I beg your pardon, Duchess," he mumbles.

"Let him go," she says, "but make sure he doesn't return."

Guards grab each of Wiets's arms and lead him away. You look around anxiously. No one has seen you. Should you follow Wiets out or stay?

*If you leave with Wiets,
turn to page 40.*

*If you remain in the castle,
turn to page 55.*

"Sorceress!" you yell toward the swirling lavender wind. "Sorceress, I need your help!"

The tornado weaves its way between trees until the last lavender wisp is out of sight. You sigh with disappointment. You're sure that was the sorceress and now you've missed your chance.

You've just resumed walking when a blur of silvery sheen catches your eye. Moving slowly between the trees is something furry. It's not exactly silver, but maybe it's a unicorn. Or could *this* be the sorceress?

As you get closer, you soon realize it's not a unicorn, but a person wrapped in silver-flecked furs. Even though the sorceress wore purple the last time you saw her, maybe this is her winter wardrobe.

Turn to the next page.

"Sorceress!" you call.

The person turns to face you. A pair of red eyes stares at you, and your heart stops. This is not the sorceress!

"Are you the warlock?" you stammer.

"No, that's my little brother you're thinking of. I believe I'm called The Witch, but I do have a name: Borah." She blinks her red eyes calmly, and your fear melts just a little.

"We aren't close," she continues, "but I need to find him now. This winter can't go on."

You sigh with relief. "You're going to tell him to end winter?" you ask.

Borah rolls her eyes. "You must not have a little brother, or you would know he won't listen to anything I say. No, I'm going to undo his ridiculous spell."

"That's great news! Thank you!" you say. "But if you're a witch, why can't you just cast a spell to end winter yourself right now?"

"Spells are tricky," says Borah. "Especially layering one spell on top of another. There are bound to be unforeseen complications. It's much wiser to undo his spell than to layer another on top of it."

You nod. You're excited to learn a little about magic!

Go on to the next page.

"There's just one problem," says Borah. "I've been wandering around Flanders for a couple of weeks now and I can't find him. He must have moved since I last saw him about 80 years ago."

"Eighty years ago? How old are you?" you can't help asking, because Borah doesn't look wizened at all.

"Let's just say there are only a few thousand-year-old oaks that are more ancient than me." She waves her arm around the forest. "All this is new. I'm not sure these trees were even here the last time I saw my brother."

"People say he's spending the winter in some ruins near the windmill. I could help you find him," you tell her.

"Thank you, that would be wonderful," says Borah. "In fact, if you don't mind becoming a spy, I need to find out more about what kind of spell he's used for extending winter. I can't undo what I don't understand."

You love the idea of becoming a spy!

"How many different kinds of spells can there be?" you ask.

Borah pauses to think. "For extending winter, I imagine he could use any number of spells. Maybe he wrote it on the earth. Maybe it's a spell of sound or a spell of breath. He could even have made all the rats in Flanders carry winter with them. It's almost certainly not an edible spell, but it could be a spell carried by water. You wouldn't have to learn every detail of the spell, just what kind it is."

Turn to the next page.

"I can do that!" Feeling very excited, you lead Borah along the banks of the river to the windmill. "Wait here! I'll come back when I know more."

Walking away from the river, you trudge toward the ruins of a stone cottage. No one has wanted to live there since the plague more than 100 years ago, but the warlock moved in at the start of winter. He says the plague has been gone for ages, and besides, he's a warlock. He's not afraid of disease and he's not afraid of ghosts.

You look around to see if the warlock is nearby. "Hello! Hello!" you call into what seems to be the entrance. Only your voice echoes back.

Do you dare to enter the home where plague killed the occupants years ago? Has enough time passed? You might find some of the warlock's magical tools, but it's probably safer to wait outside for him to show up.

If you step inside the collapsed cottage, turn to page 105.

If you think it's better to wait outside for the warlock's return, turn to page 56.

"Let me tell you a story," you tell the warlock. You stop walking and turn to face him.

The warlock looks skeptical but says nothing.

"Once upon a time, there was a small village along a river in Flanders. People have lived there for hundreds of years, but this story begins more recently, maybe 70 or 80 years ago, when a unicorn appeared carrying a little girl."

"She was riding the unicorn?" the warlock asks.

"She was too young to know how to ride properly, so she really just sat on the unicorn's back and clutched the mane. Her hair was almost as pale as the unicorn's fur, and all her clothing was white. To everyone's surprise, the child only spoke French, which means she must have traveled a great distance from France. No one could understand anything she said, except that her name was Marie-Claire."

Turn to the next page.

"What happened to the unicorn?" asks the warlock.

"Later that day, as soon as Marie-Claire was adopted by a couple without children, the unicorn disappeared, but for many years, the villagers called her the unicorn girl. All this took place when Marie-Claire was so young that she's never been able to explain what happened. Some people say the unicorn rescued her from some tragedy, but

others say she's the ghost of another unicorn. Then there are other people who think she was a unicorn transformed into a human child."

The warlock scowls. "Why would anyone think that?"

"Well, for many years, when Marie-Claire was outside around twilight, you could see a shadowy image of a unicorn near her. A ghost unicorn! You couldn't touch this unicorn. In fact, if you tried to, your hand would go right through as if it were a cloud."

Go on to the next page.

You pause to pull your hat down over your ears, which are now beginning to freeze.

"The mysterious thing is, once Marie-Claire married, the ghost unicorn was never seen again!"

The warlock grins. "That's a good story!"

"I'm not done," you say. "Marie-Claire still lives in the village. She's the oldest person there. She knows a million things about healing, so she's very important to us. This unending winter has been very hard on her health. I'm afraid she'll die. Even if she doesn't, it looks like the snow might cause her roof to collapse and then she'll be homeless. But the big problem is that everyone in the village is going to run out of food very soon. We really need to plant our spring crops or this will definitely be Marie-Claire's last winter."

You look at the warlock expectantly.

Turn to page 82.

36

You listen carefully to the soft whimpers and walk in that direction. Not far away, you come to a young unicorn with its leg caught in a trap!

You want to throw your arms around the poor creature, but are careful not to scare it. Approaching slowly, you speak to it gently.

"I'll help you. I'm your friend," you say. "This will be okay." You hope you're right about that!

You carefully open the trap. The unicorn's leg is badly injured, and silvery blood puddles in the snow. As you tenderly pat the unicorn to console it, you notice its tears have a silvery glow.

If it weren't winter, you could look for spiderwebs and yarrow leaves to apply to the unicorn's wound. Now you know the best you can hope for is getting the unicorn to Marie-Claire; she's known for her herbs and healing. You try to help the unicorn up, but it whinnies in pain. It can't even stand, never mind walk.

Turn to page 38.

As gently as you can, you hoist the unicorn onto your back, then take a few staggering steps. This unicorn is young, but it's still bigger and heavier than any dog you've ever seen. Carrying it back toward the village exhausts you.

While you trudge through the snow, you remember the unicorn's silver blood and silver tears. Even though its fur is white, could this be a silver unicorn? You look over your shoulder at its eyes. They're pale gray. *Just how silver does a unicorn have to be to satisfy the warlock?* you wonder.

By the time you reach Marie-Claire's cottage, you are panting and drenched with sweat, but at least the unicorn has stopped crying.

When Marie-Claire opens the door, her jaw drops. She ushers you inside and helps you lay the injured unicorn on her bed. You wash the wound while she mixes healing herbs. Then she sets the bone and bandages the unicorn's leg.

"Did you notice the silver blood?" you ask Marie-Claire. "Do you think this unicorn will grow up to be a silver unicorn?"

Go on to the next page.

At first, Marie-Claire doesn't answer. She examines the unicorn's eyes and fingers its mane and tail. "All unicorns have silver blood, and silver tears as well, but this one does have strands of silver hair. Also, those pale gray eyes . . . I don't know if this is the child of one silver unicorn parent, or if this is what a silver unicorn looks like when it's young."

The young unicorn is sleeping peacefully. You tenderly stroke its head.

"In a few days, once this unicorn is in better shape, I could bring it to the warlock," you tell Marie-Claire. "He might think it's silver enough."

"You could. Even though unicorns heal much more quickly than we do, it will still be a few days until this one can walk," she says. "You could also see if you can find this unicorn's parents. At least one of them might be silver."

You feel torn. On one hand, you hate the idea of giving this young unicorn to the warlock. Yet on the other, you know you'd prefer to spend the next few days at the bedside of this unicorn rather than out in the cold looking for a grown silver unicorn.

If you decide to stay with this unicorn until it's well enough to take to the warlock, turn to page 58.

If you decide to return to the forest to look for a silver unicorn, turn to page 129.

With your head down, you sheepishly follow Wiets out of the castle.

"I'm sorry. That didn't work out the way I thought it would," he admits.

"That's okay. I don't think the warlock really wants a toy unicorn anyway, but now I have to look for a silver unicorn in the forest."

Wiets nods. "I'll help you."

The snow in the forest is deep and undisturbed. Making your way through it is so much slower than skating, but it gives you a chance to look at the birds huddled together on branches and the acrobatic squirrels leaping from one tree to another.

You've walked for a couple of hours when Wiets points and says, "Look through the trees ahead. Is that a wall?"

As you get closer, you see that it *is* a wall of sorts, but a dense wall of thorns, each the length of your pinky and tipped with silver. You and Wiets explore the wall and discover it's circular. Looking up, you see that the tower of thorns grazes the treetops.

"I wonder what's inside," you say, peering between the thorns.

The mesh of thorns is so thick that it's hard to see much inside except a flash of silver. You press your face closer, and a thorn tears open the skin below your eye.

Turn to page 42.

"Be careful!" Wiets warns, blotting your blood with his mitten.

"I saw something silver inside!" you tell him.

"A unicorn?"

"I couldn't tell."

Wiets squints his eyes to look through the thorns. "There's definitely something silver in there and I saw it move. We're going in!"

"Are you crazy?" you ask with astonishment. The scratch on your face is starting to sting. "We'll be ripped to shreds if we force our way in."

Without a word, Wiets pulls a small knife from his pocket.

You raise an eyebrow skeptically. "That knife is hardly bigger than the thorns. It will take forever to cut a hole."

Wiets ignores you and starts slicing away near the base of the wall.

"Ow!" he shouts. He pulls off his mitten and puts a bleeding finger in his mouth. He hands you the knife.

You do your best to cut the thorny branches without piercing your own skin, but it's impossible to avoid. There are blood spots all over your mittens. You and Wiets take turns cutting branches and nursing the wounds that result.

Finally, when you are elbow-deep in thorns, you say, "I'm almost through!" Just as you cut the last section of a narrow tunnel through the thorns and withdraw your arm, you hear scurrying sounds and a silvery mouse races out and burrows into the snow.

Go on to the next page.

You and Wiets are looking at each other, open-mouthed with surprise, when a second silver mouse emerges from the thorns.

"Should we keep going?" he asks. "I don't feel like getting all cut up just for mice, even if they *are* silver."

A third silver mouse emerges and skitters across the snow. You chase it, hoping for a closer look.

Then you stop in your tracks. "Wiets," you call, "there are hoofprints here! They're too small for a horse."

"Could they be deer prints?" he asks.

You roll your eyes. "I know what deer prints look like. I think these might be unicorn prints!"

"Do you want to follow the tracks or continue cutting our way through the thorns?" he asks.

If you decide to continue creating an entrance through the tunnel of thorns, turn to page 51.

If you decide to follow the tracks, turn to page 79.

As you follow the silver birds, you try not think about the cries of pain you're leaving behind. The birds are flying faster than you can stumble through the snow. Even though you move as quickly as you can, you worry that you'll lose track of them.

You're panting with exhaustion when the birds finally land on a tree, but not an ordinary winter-bare tree. This one has a remarkably silver trunk and glistening branches. You pull off a mitten to run your palm against it. The trunk even smells metallic. It's true that you're not familiar with every tree in the forest outside your village, but how is it possible you've never seen this one? Why haven't your neighbors ever spoken of a silver tree?

You examine it closely. The trunk has a vertical opening that's almost your height. As you trace the edge with your finger, you notice a bit of torn purple silk snagged on the wood. Could this be where the sorceress lives now? Purple is her color, and none of the villagers can afford clothing like that.

Go on to the next page.

"Sorceress!" you call into the opening. "Sorceress, are you there?"

The only response is the slight tinny echo of your voice. Still, you can't help thinking the sorceress has something to do with this tree. You might be able to squeeze inside the opening. What would you find inside? Would it lead to the sorceress's home?

As you think about that possibility, the chattering of the silver birds makes you look up to the boughs. Could those branches be solid silver? If so, each branch is worth a fortune! You don't have any way of cutting an entire branch off, but what if you snapped off the smallest twigs? Even a handful of silver twigs would make it possible for you to buy food for yourself and Marie-Claire. There's not a lot of food left in the village, but with enough silver, you could travel to Bruges. Surely there's food in the city that you could buy and bring back.

You're excited! You feel like you have two promising possibilities. Should you try to step inside the tree and see if it leads to the sorceress's home, or try to break off silver twigs from the tree?

If you climb inside the tree,
turn to page 95.

If you decide to snap off the smallest silver branches, turn to page 98.

46

"Come with me to my village. We can stop there on the way to the silver unicorn. We could warm up before continuing our journey," you say to the warlock. You try to muster a welcoming smile, even though part of you wonders if this is really a good idea. You tell yourself the warlock will surely end winter when he sees how badly the villagers are suffering.

The warlock turns his red eyes to the sky, then slowly scans the forest around you. He shrugs. "Sure, let's go. I wouldn't mind a snack if it's not too far out of the way."

A snack? Doesn't he realize the villagers are starving?

You turn toward home, wondering what on earth you'll be able to find for a snack. You hear the warlock panting behind you.

Go on to the next page.

At the edge of the forest, where the snowy fields of your village begin, you pause. You can see your neighbors walking in the lanes between cottages, and you yearn to be home.

"Come on, we're almost there!" you call to the warlock.

As you approach the village, you notice your neighbors have stopped moving. They're just standing watching you. You wave your hand in greeting, but no one waves back.

"Hi, it's me!" you shout.

Then a snowball hits you in the chest! You realize everyone is making snowballs, and soon you're pummeled by snow.

Turn to the next page.

Should you continue on? You've come this far with the warlock, so you hate to give up now. However, this is not exactly a warm welcome.

"They're just having fun with snowballs," you tell the warlock. When he catches up to you, you take his hand and step forward.

Suddenly, a rock hits the warlock!

He drops your hand and snarls like a wolf. "Who dares to attack the warlock? Now you'll find out just how fierce winter can be!"

"Noooooo!" you cry, but it's too late.

The warlock wraps his arms to his chest, then turns in circles, faster and faster, until he's spinning with inhuman speed. He abruptly stops and his arms fly open, unleashing a terrible blizzard!

The wind howls and the temperature plunges. The snow is blinding. You can't open your eyes enough to find your way home. In just minutes, you are completely encased in ice.

The warlock eventually ends winter everywhere except for your village. No one there survives, and people in Flanders call it "The Place of Eternal Winter." In summer, a few brave people come to get some snow to cool their drinks, but most of the time, everyone stays far, far away.

The End

The fox barks again as you pivot away from it. You're not going to be tricked by a fox!

You walk through the silent forest without any clear direction. As the woods grow dark and shadowy, you realize you should turn back and follow your footprints to the castle. Surely the guards would at least let you sleep in the courtyard tonight.

The only trouble is, you've misjudged how long it takes to reach the castle. Under the black and moonless sky, you can't see your footprints anymore. You're going to have to spend the night in the forest!

You drag some fallen limbs to the base of a large tree. They probably won't keep you warm, but they at least provide a sense of shelter. You burrow into the snow beneath them, knowing this will probably be the worst night of your life. In fact, it could be the *last* night of your life!

Turn to the next page.

50

Your hands and feet are stinging with cold. Soon you can't feel your nose. You curl into a tight ball and stick your hands into opposite armpits. Your teeth chatter and every muscle tightens. Despite this, you feel yourself drifting to sleep, or maybe to death.

At some point you sense a mass of heat along your back. Something warm and moist moves across your cheek. A horse—no, it's a unicorn—is licking your face!

Am I dead or am I dreaming? you wonder and close your eyes.

You're dreaming, but it's the final dream of your young life.

The End

You cut thorns to widen the opening, and then Wiets takes a turn. Every now and then, another silver mouse scurries out. You notice Wiets's eyebrows have become silvery, although maybe it's just frost. The opening slowly expands until it's wide enough for your shoulders to fit through.

You lie on your belly and wriggle through the tunnel of thorns, trying not to scratch your face. The thorns snag on your hat and your sleeves, and occasionally you feel one tear your cheek. Wiets follows behind you.

Turn to the next page.

You are only halfway through when you see four silver legs standing inside. You lift your head and gasp!

There's a silver unicorn!

Breathlessly, you pull your way through the thorns and grab Wiets's hand to help him after you.

You're speechless with wonder as you gaze at the unicorn. Turning to tell Wiets how thrilled you are, you see that not just his eyebrows, but the hair on his head is now entirely silver! He's looking at you in shock.

"Your hair," he stammers. He takes hold of a silvery strand. "It's so beautiful!"

The silver unicorn comes over to gently nudge your hand.

Turn to the next page.

"Well, never mind our hair," you say as you run your fingers through the unicorn's mane. "At least we found a silver unicorn. We'll have to make the tunnel a lot bigger to get this creature out."

Wiets isn't listening. He's walking along the thorny wall of the tower, looking perplexed.

"Where *is* the tunnel?"

You turn in panic to look. "It was right behind you, but now it's completely closed up again!"

Wiets sighs. "Okay, we'll have to cut another tunnel." He pats his pockets, and horror fills his face.

"I left my knife outside. I was afraid I would accidentally stab myself when I wiggled through."

"You mean we're stuck here?" you ask.

Wiets nods, and the unicorn nuzzles your tears.

The End

You gaze at Wiets until he's gone. Your heart is pounding as you emerge from behind the shield and approach the woman. Wiets called her "Duchess," but is she?

Bowing your head, you say, "I'm a new servant. I'm not sure where to go."

The woman lifts your chin with her finger and studies your face. You try to appear calm.

"What work were you hired for?" she asks.

You can't believe you have a choice! You have to think quickly. The work you are best at, and which you enjoy most, is sewing. That would keep you indoors and give you a chance to explore the castle. However, if there is a real silver unicorn, and not just a small statue, working in the stable would give you the best access to the creature.

If you say, "I'm known for my needlework,"
turn to page 83.

If you say, "I'm meant to work in the stable,"
turn to page 96.

You stand outside the remains of a cottage while you wait for the warlock to return. Luckily, it's only a matter of minutes before you see a man in a red hat scurrying between the trees toward you. When you see his red eyes, even brighter than his hat, you're sure it's the warlock.

"What are you doing here?" he asks suspiciously.

"Because of you, I've been thrown out of my village," you tell him. You sniffle and pretend to cry.

"Because of me?"

"Everyone in my village is mad at you for extending winter. I keep telling them you must have a good reason and that you're not just being cruel. They said if I think so highly of you, I should go live with you, so here I am. Can I be your assistant?"

The warlock scowls. "I don't need an assistant."

"You must have a lot to do," you insist. "I could help you!" Of course, the idea of spending much time with him sends chills up your spine! You really hope you don't have to go inside the pile of stones that used to be a cottage.

The warlock looks skeptical.

"Pleeeeease!" you beg.

"Well," he says, "my home is a bit of a mess. I suppose you could clean it."

Go on to the next page.

You hesitate. It's been more than a century since the plague killed the people who lived here, but going inside is still very spooky. You remind yourself you offered to be a spy, so you have to be brave! Ducking your head, you step into what remains of the cottage. Fallen stones lie everywhere and a thin dusting of dirt coats everything. You start by straightening out a pile of animal skins that you assume is the warlock's bed, but the place really needs to be swept. You look around for a broom. What are you supposed to clean with?

You could tell the warlock you need to gather pine boughs to make a broom, and use that opportunity to check in with Borah. But the warlock wasn't so enthusiastic about having you around to start with. If you leave, even temporarily, will he allow you back? Will he think you're shirking your job?

If you tell the warlock you need to get pine boughs to make a broom, turn to page 66.

If you think it's better not to leave yet, turn to page 89.

58

You stay by the young unicorn's side as it recovers. Marie-Claire makes an herbal broth to speed up healing, and you spoon it gently into the unicorn's mouth. You sing lullabies and comb its mane. When you touch the unicorn, it makes a sweet purring sound, just like a kitten's.

"You're falling in love with that creature," Marie-Claire warns. "How are you ever going to give it to the warlock?"

You know she's right, but it's too late. You *already* love the unicorn with your entire heart!

Go on to the next page.

After a few days, the unicorn is able to stand, and the next morning, Marie-Claire announces that it will be able to walk to the warlock's cottage. For you, it's heartbreaking news.

Marie-Claire hugs you and whispers, "This might be the hardest thing you've ever had to do! Be brave, and know that you're saving the village!" She ties a leash around the unicorn's neck and hands the other end to you.

You're crying as you lead the young unicorn out of Marie-Claire's cottage, through the village, and into the forest. Your sobs fill the snowy silence of the woods. When you stop to make sure the unicorn is okay, you notice silver tears dripping from its face. Does the unicorn know what's going to happen or is it crying in sympathy with you?

Turn to the next page.

60

When you reach the ruins of a stone cottage where the warlock is said to live, you shout, "Warlock! Warlock! I have a silver unicorn for you!" Your voice is choked with tears.

The warlock scrambles out of what looks like a pile of rocks. He blinks his red eyes and gazes at the unicorn.

"It's not really silver," he comments.

Hope fills your heart. Maybe he won't want this unicorn after all!

The warlock comes closer to touch the unicorn's mane and the creature flinches. "It's sort of silvery," he says.

He uses two fingers to widen one eye of the frightened unicorn. "I suppose these eyes might turn silver."

You will yourself to say, "This is what a silver unicorn looks like when it's young. It will get more silvery with age." Of course, you have no idea if that's true.

The warlock nods and takes the rope from your hand. You squeeze your eyes shut to stop your tears as you say, "End the winter. End it now."

Go on to the next page.

The warlock loops the leash around his wrist and begins clapping his hands so quickly that you can barely catch the rhythm. Then you realize the rhythm is so strange and complicated that it's more like language than music.

By the time he stops, snow has melted around your boots. You feel warm enough to pull off your hat and use it to wipe your tears.

When you hug the unicorn goodbye, you start crying all over again. "Please take very good care of this creature!" you beg the warlock. The unicorn makes a heart-wrenching sob as you turn away and walk home.

The next few days are busy with preparing the soil and planting spring crops, but you feel nothing but sadness. The villagers thank you for ending winter, and you try to smile, but your heart is broken. You can't stop thinking about the young unicorn.

Turn to page 63.

About a week later, you can't stand it anymore. Without telling anyone, you leave the village at sunrise and head toward the warlock's home. What a different walk this is now! The snow is gone, and the ground is soggy. Leaves are just beginning to unfurl, and songbirds are singing of love. You are too glum to even notice.

You reach the clearing where you remember leaving the unicorn with the warlock, but it's different, and for a moment you wonder if you've come to the right place. The ruins have been reassembled into a stone cottage with wildflowers already blooming by the door. When you peer in a window, you see piles of fresh hay. *Could this be a stable for the unicorn?* you wonder.

The sound of a lilting song catches your attention. The warlock saunters around the corner of the cottage with his arm draped affectionately over the young unicorn.

He stops when he sees you. "What are you doing here? Did you come to steal my unicorn back?" He hugs the unicorn protectively, and to your surprise, the unicorn nuzzles his face.

Turn to the next page.

"No, no," you insist. "I just wanted to make sure the unicorn is okay."

The warlock grins. "Well, have a look!"

The unicorn glows with vitality. Its coat has a silvery sheen, and the warlock places a small wreath of wildflowers around its horn. When you reach your hand toward the unicorn, it shyly turns its head to the warlock's chest. You can't help feeling a little jealous that the unicorn seems to have forgotten you and is now so attached to the warlock.

"I'm not sure this really is a silver unicorn," he tells you, "but I don't care. This little unicorn has changed my life. Look, I built a stable and I made wildflowers grow so there is plenty of fresh, sweet food."

Go on to the next page.

He kisses the unicorn's forehead and the creature whinnies with delight.

"All right," you say, and force yourself to smile. "I can see you two are doing fine together."

You wave goodbye and walk home. You try to enjoy the sunshine on your shoulders, but you fight back tears the entire way.

Back in the village, you find Marie-Claire poking seeds into her garden. She takes one look at you and opens her arms for a hug. Between sobs, you tell her about the warlock and the unicorn.

"I know I got the warlock to end winter, and I know the young unicorn has a good home," you say, "but I'm so sad about losing the unicorn."

Marie-Claire pats your back and says, "You need a new adventure, and I have an idea."

You start to smile . . .

The End

When you step outside the ruined cottage, the warlock says, "You can't be finished already!"

You reply, "No, I'm not. I need a broom. I'm going to gather some evergreen branches to make something to sweep with."

He looks at you suspiciously.

As you head back toward the windmill where Borah waits, you whistle a cheerful tune so she will hear you approaching. You're excited to be a spy, and optimistic that you'll be part of the magic that ends the winter. You imagine how grateful the villagers will be.

When you reach the windmill, Borah steps out of the shadows and says, "You're back already?"

Before you can answer, something lands on your back, knocking you to the ground. Your face is jammed into the snow.

"Borah!" you hear the warlock exclaim, and you realize it's him who is pinning you to the ground.

"Get off the child!" says Borah icily.

The warlock stands, yanking you up with him. His hot hand is tight around your throat. It's very hard to breathe and you start to panic.

Turn to page 68.

68

"Why are you here, Borah?" the warlock demands, and gives your neck a forceful shake.

"I'm trying to talk some sense into you," she replies. "Are you trying to kill everyone in Flanders? This winter has got to end."

"It will end when I get a silver unicorn!" he insists.

At this point, you're choking. You try to pry the warlock's hands off your neck, but he's much more powerful than you.

Go on to the next page.

Borah sighs with exasperation. "There *are* no silver unicorns, you fool! Don't make me unleash my full power. You know very well that my magic is stronger than yours, little brother!"

You wave your hands frantically, trying to get Borah's attention.

Before the warlock can answer, Borah places her hands over his. You feel the pressure around your neck weaken. The warlock howls and releases you.

You collapse onto your knees and take deep gulps of air. When you look up, you see the warlock is shaking his arms in the air. His hands seem to have melted into fingerless knobs of flesh, and his howls have turned to screeches of rage.

Borah helps you to your feet and puts her arm around you.

Turn to the next page.

"Winter will never end now!" shouts the warlock. "It was a clapping spell, and now I don't have hands to undo it!"

Borah laughs. "Yes, but I do, and now that I know it's a clapping spell, I can end winter myself."

Even though the warlock tried to kill you, you can't help asking Borah, "How can he live without hands?"

Borah puts her other arm around the warlock. "He's my responsibility now, just like when he was a kid. It's going to be up to me to keep him out of trouble."

"That doesn't sound like fun," you tell her.

Borah rolls her red eyes. "A big sister's work is never fun, never done. Go on home. By the time you get there, spring will be starting."

The End

"I'm coming," you tell the fox. The creature turns and scampers deeper into the forest.

With each of your footsteps sinking deep into the snow, it's impossible to keep up with the fox. However, whenever you think you're lost, you spot some red and realize the fox is waiting for you. As the sky darkens, the fox slows its pace. You're starting to wonder how you will spend the night in a freezing forest when the fox stops beside a burrow in the snow.

The fox barks, and it sounds like "In."

You peer into the hole and see that it's a tunnel. "No, no, no," you reply. "This looks like a trap. I am not going in first!"

The fox swishes its tail, enters the burrow, and disappears.

Turn to the next page.

You feel certain there's no silver unicorn in that tunnel, but it might at least be a warm place to spend the night. Even though this makes you very nervous, you scramble onto your hands and knees to crawl into the burrow.

It's too dark to see anything. The tunnel has the sharp tangy smell of fox. You crawl until your hand brushes fox fur and you hear a high-pitched yip. Sitting back on your heels, you realize you've come to a larger space, a fox den. As your eyes adjust to the darkness, you see six pairs of eyes. Five of them are very small.

You reach out a hand and your fingers find the ears of a baby fox. You watch its eyes blink. When you scratch the fox kit's head, you hear purring, just like a cat's! You pick up the kit and hold it to your chest, then with your other arm, bring a second fox kit to you. A third curls around your knees. You're feeling warm and cozy! Even though you still haven't found a silver unicorn, you're so glad you followed the fox into this den. You yawn as you feel your body relax.

Go on to the next page.

You lie down with five fox kits cuddled around you. The adult fox curls against your back. It's like sleeping draped in furs! Almost immediately, you fall into a dreamless sleep.

You have no idea how long you sleep. You awake to fox kits prodding your belly. Now it's so much easier to see in the fox den, almost as if candles have been lit, so you can look carefully at the cute baby foxes for the first time. You move your arm to reach for one, but are astonished to see that your arm has become a fox leg!

Turn to the next page.

"What???" you yell, but the sound is the screech of a fox.

When the adult fox barks back, you understand perfectly that the mother fox was killed by a hunter and these babies need a mom.

"But I'm not a fox!"

"You are now," the fox replies. "Once you sleep in a fox den, you become a fox. Everyone knows that!"

You didn't. Even though you never expected to become a fox, you've got five kits desperate for your care, and suddenly you love them. It turns out foxes don't think about silver unicorns at all.

The End

You know you've reached the Stream of Lost Memories when you come to a shallow river of deep blue water. There's even a bit of steam rising from it. "We have to wade across," you tell the warlock. "There's no bridge, but the water looks shallow." There's something almost mesmerizing about the water. Have you ever seen anything so blue?

The warlock stands beside you at the edge of the stream. "This isn't frozen. That means it's enchanted." He pokes you and says, "You go first."

There's no way you're going to step into the Stream of Lost Memories!

Turn to the next page.

You take a deep breath, then, with all the power you can muster, shove the warlock into the stream. He's quick, however, and stronger than you, so when he grabs you, both of your bodies splash into the warm water. You spit out some water, sit up, and wipe water from your eyes.

Beside you, the warlock is floating on his back. He's smiling. Then he rolls over in the water and sits up. "Remind me why we're here," he says.

You look at him in confusion. You have no idea why you're here either. You remember he's the warlock, but why are you sitting in a stream with him? Is he your friend?

The warlock watches you climb out of the stream onto the snowy bank. Your wet body is freezing!

Turn to the next page.

"I'm tired of snow," he announces, "and I don't want to be cold when I get out of the water." He claps his hands and drops of enchanted water fly into the air. He continues clapping a weird beat that stops and starts with no apparent rhythm.

You hug yourself and rub your arms to warm up. The sunlight seems stronger now. You wring water out of your hat and hair, then pause. Is that the sound of birds singing? You squeeze water from your shawl and flap it to dry it out. The air is definitely warming up.

"I'm going home now," you tell the warlock, and you search your mind to remember where home is. With a sinking feeling, you realize you've forgotten where you live.

Winter ends, but you never find your way home.

The End

"Let's follow the tracks," you whisper, "but we should be very quiet."

Wiets nods and gestures for you to go first. As silently as you can, you step through the snow alongside the hoofprints.

They lead to a glittering silvery web stretched between branches. You look through the web to find a white unicorn nibbling lichen from a tree trunk.

You gasp with excitement. Behind you, a cheerful voice says, "I think this spell will work!"

You spin around to find a very wrinkled woman draped in a splendid purple velvet robe.

No one you know wears velvet of any color, never mind purple. "Are you the sorceress?" you ask shyly.

"Indeed!" she exclaims. "And thank you! It's nice to be recognized."

"What are you doing with the unicorn?" asks Wiets.

"You've probably heard about the warlock's crazy desire," the sorceress tells you. "I'm trying to turn this unicorn silver, so we can be done with this winter once and for all. Unfortunately, my first attempt with the silver thorns didn't go so well."

"The tower of silver-tipped thorns?" you ask.

The sorceress nods. "There's a unicorn inside that tower, and I'm pretty sure it turned silver, but I can't get that creature out!"

"We can help you!" Wiets shows her his knife.

Turn to the next page.

80

The sorceress reaches into her own pockets and with each hand pulls out a gleaming silver knife. "Even magic knives can't keep the thorns from closing up. Trust me, I've given up on that project, but you can give me a hand with this web."

Each of you takes a corner of the fragile web, and the fourth corner remains attached to a branch. Very carefully, you drape it over the anxious unicorn. You whisper to the unicorn to calm it down. Then the sorceress starts chanting in a language you can't understand and flutters her hands expressively. The unicorn whinnies, and gradually, its fur takes on a metallic sheen. The silver web evaporates.

"You did it!" you exclaim to the sorceress. When you stroke the strange silvery mane of the unicorn, it rubs its nose against your cheek.

Go on to the next page.

The sorceress modestly bows her head and says, "I'm grateful for your help. I'm afraid I'm going to need another favor from you. I can get myself home in one purple swoosh of a wind, but magically moving a unicorn is not something I know how to do."

"We'll help!" you offer eagerly. "We can take turns riding and leading the unicorn."

"Thank you!" says the sorceress. "Take the unicorn home for the night and we'll meet tomorrow morning to take it to the warlock. This winter will finally end!"

By the following evening, most of the snow has melted. Trees have sprouted fat buds and birds are welcoming spring with song. You are so happy that you sing too.

The End

"I suppose I could end winter, but there's one condition," he says. "You need to visit me every day to tell me a story."

Your heart sinks. "Every day?"

"Every day," he insists. "If you miss one day, I'll bring back winter."

"Okay," you agree. "I'll meet you here tomorrow."

Even though having to tell a story to the warlock every day sounds awful, you remind yourself at least you've saved your village, and maybe all of Flanders, from the winter without end. As the days pass, you start to enjoy thinking up stories, and you practice telling them first to your neighbors. Everyone loves your tales, and people offer to take over your farm chores so you can focus on creating stories. Your life as a storyteller has begun!

The End

"You're here to sew?" asks a servant. "Come with me."

As she leads you through the castle, she introduces herself as Nan, the head seamstress. "I can see you're cold, and you must be hungry. Let's get you some hot soup before you start sewing."

You follow Nan into a kitchen with steaming pots and the sounds of several servants chopping vegetables. They glance at you with curiosity. Nan introduces you and ladles out a bowl of soup.

You wrap your numb fingers around the warm bowl. For a moment, you forget about the silver unicorn, you forget about Wiets, and you think you would be very happy to live in this castle and sew. Your heart slows as you gratefully drink the soup.

When you're finished, Nan takes you to a narrow room lined with windows. Several women and girls are bent over their stitching but look up to welcome you.

"You'll start by hemming the new bed linens," says Nan, "and then I'll see how you do."

You nod your head, take a needle, and get to work. Even though this is the most boring, undemanding sewing possible, you take tiny stitches. Each one is perfect. You understand that unless you impress Nan, you'll be hemming bed linens for a long time.

When you finish, Nan inspects your work. "Quite nice!" she exclaims. "How are you at fitting dresses?"

Turn to the next page.

You gulp. Because no one in the village wears fancy clothes, you have no experience with that at all!

"Actually," you tell her, "embroidery is my specialty."

Nan raises her eyebrows. "All right. Embroider the pillowcases. Let me see your best work." She hands you a basket filled with spools of silk thread. You rummage through, admiring the jewel-like colors, and are surprised to discover there's silver thread. You've never seen that before!

Go on to the next page.

Even though all the unicorns you've ever encountered have been white, the bright silk threads inspire you to embroider a rainbow parade of unicorns, each with a silver horn. Some of the unicorns are prancing, others are standing on their hind legs, and every now and then, you create a unicorn with tiny wings. The hours pass until candles are lit and you have to squint to see your smallest stitches. Nan holds up your embroidery near the flame and gasps.

"This is spectacular! No wonder the Duke sent for you to work here!"

You try to appear modest, but you're bursting with pride. Of course, you don't tell her the Duke didn't hire you!

"Tomorrow," says Nan, "you'll finish the pillowcases, and then you'll embroider the new vest we're making for the Duke's return."

That night, even though you are just a servant, you receive a bigger meal than you've eaten since the winter solstice. You sleep under heavy woolen blankets in a room warmed by the breath of the other seamstresses. Your dreams are full of unicorns, but not one is silver.

Turn to the next page.

86

The next afternoon, Nan brings you a deep blue vest. It is already trimmed with a silver braid. "The Duke has been gone for a month already," she explains. "The Duchess wants a special gift for when he finally returns. Do you have a design in mind or shall I suggest one?"

You touch the silk. It's so fine that it seems to melt under your fingers. "What do you think about a herd of silver unicorns galloping up one side and down the other?"

Nan claps her hands with delight. "He'll love that!"

"Just one thing," you say, "I've never actually seen a silver unicorn. If the Duke has one, it would help me to see it first so I get the shape right."

Nan rolls her eyes. "Oh, please! You just embroidered dozens of unicorns on those pillowcases. Silver unicorns look just like regular unicorns except for their color. Now start working. The Duke could arrive home any day, and we want to be ready."

You are about to ask Nan how she knows what a silver unicorn looks like, but she looks at you impatiently and gestures toward the basket of thread.

Turn to page 88.

Your work is precise, but quick. You empty your mind, so that all you think about is each stitch you are taking. When Nan announces that the day is over and it's time to eat, you look up with surprise.

As the days pass, the vest becomes more and more glorious. Even the Duchess comes in to admire it.

The vest is nearly done—there are 108 unicorns, you count—when you get an idea. What if you brought this silver unicorn–covered vest to the warlock? Surely over 100 tiny silver unicorns would delight him enough to end winter. On the other hand, you still haven't found out if there's a silver unicorn in the Duke's stable. As much as you've enjoyed embroidering unicorns, you remind yourself that you really need to find one, or else satisfy the warlock with something else.

If you take the unicorn-covered vest to the warlock, turn to page 101.

If you stay to investigate the stable, turn to page 106.

You do your best to wipe what seems to be a crude table with your shawl and push dirt into a corner with your foot. The warlock's home isn't exactly clean, but you've made it a little tidier, and you're eager to get out of this possibly plague-ridden place. You step outside and gratefully inhale fresh air.

The warlock is perched on a nearby stone examining a dead squirrel in his hands.

"I could cook that for you!" you suggest.

The warlock snorts. "I don't need a cook. Watch this."

Turn to the next page.

You gasp with horror as he slices open the squirrel fur with one sharp fingernail and rips the skin off, tossing the fur to the side. He places the squirrel body on the snow and squats beside it. Then he holds his hands over the squirrel and begins rapidly clapping. It's a strange rhythm, much too irregular to keep track of. The snow around the squirrel quickly melts and the flesh starts to sizzle.

"That's amazing!" you say. "I can't believe you can cook just by clapping."

"It's not *just* clapping," the warlock corrects you. "It's a clapping spell. In fact, that's how I extended winter. Clapping controls temperature."

You can't believe your ears! You pick up the bloody squirrel skin and say, "I can see you don't need a cook. Why don't I take care of cleaning this up for you where it won't make a mess?"

You trudge through the snow back toward the mill where Borah is waiting. Before you can even tell her what you learned, she says, "Great job! Now I know what to do!"

"I didn't even tell you!"

Go on to the next page.

"My hearing is much better than yours," Borah explains. "I can undo a clapping spell myself, but we need to figure out a way to stop him from clapping winter back again."

"What about mittens?" you ask, pulling off your own. "Mittens would muffle the sound. Can you make mittens he can't take off?"

Borah nods her head thoughtfully. "This could work. No offense, but your own mittens are pretty shabby. Let's spruce them up with some of the squirrel fur and then I can make sure they won't ever come off his hands."

It's messy work and your fingers are freezing, but you manage to work tufts of squirrel fur into your own mittens. Borah uses strands of her own silvery hair to bind the squirrel tail along the edge of each mitten. The result isn't half bad.

You return to the warlock and present the mittens. "I made you fur mittens," you tell him proudly.

Turn to the next page.

The warlock is startled. He grabs the mittens and examines them carefully. "You made these for me?"

"I did! I can see how important your hands are, so you should protect them when you aren't clapping."

The warlock smiles shyly as he slides the mittens on his hands. "No one ever gives me gifts. Thank you!"

You want to be far away when the warlock discovers the mittens won't ever come off, so you say, "I have some other things I'm working on. I'll be back in a while." You hurry back to Borah.

"I'm impressed!" she says. "My brother may not have wanted you for an assistant, but I do! Come work with me and I'll teach you every bit of magic I know, starting with how to clap winter away. Would you like that?"

"I would!" you exclaim, and that afternoon you learn how clap magic into the world.

The End

You stumble through the snow and throw your body into the purple tornado.

"Magic Mother of Merlin! What was that?" you hear right before your body explodes into thousands of tiny pieces. For a second, a bit of your brain understands what must be happening, but then that bit collides with a minuscule portion of your chin, and your world goes dark.

The End

Squeezing inside the tree is going to be a very tight fit.

You start by taking off your shawl to make yourself a little smaller. You reach one arm inside, and then cram a shoulder in. Putting one leg in is easy, but getting your hip in takes a lot of wriggling. To make the rest of your torso fit, you first exhale all the air in your lungs, then shimmy more of your chest in. Your tunic snags on the edge of the opening. With this much of your chest squeezed into the tree, you can only take shallow breaths. You try to wriggle more of your body in, but suddenly you realize you're stuck!

A wave of panic washes over you. Maybe this wasn't a good idea after all. You try to remove yourself from the tree, but you can't budge in either direction. You decide to free yourself by squirming out of your clothing. You struggle to pull yourself free of your tunic, but you can't even manage that!

Now you shout for help. The metal tree is icy cold and your shawl is lying on the ground. Your tears freeze on your face, and your fingers go numb.

Years later, when people find this tree, they're amazed to see what appears to be a silver statue of someone emerging from the tree. They wonder who the artist was, not realizing it was your death.

The End

"If you're going to work in the stable, you must be very gentle with my unicorn," says the woman.

"I love unicorns!" you exclaim. *Could this unicorn possibly be silver?* you wonder.

In the stable, you introduce yourself to Josef, the stable master.

"I've heard the Duke has a silver unicorn," you say.

Josef shrugs. "You heard wrong. That's something the Duke wants very badly, and maybe when he finally returns here, he'll bring one."

"When do you expect the Duke back?" you ask Josef.

He laughs. "That's not the kind of thing the Duke tells me! He's been gone about a month already, and I'm told the Duchess is starting to worry. Now, enough about the Duke and Duchess, there are stalls for you to clean out."

You try to conceal your disappointment. "The Duchess told me to be very gentle with her unicorn. May I have a look?"

"Certainly! She's in the third stall on the right."

Go on to the next page.

You gasp at the sight of the unicorn. Even in the shadows of the stable, the unicorn glows like moonlight. A blue satin ribbon spirals up her horn, and her tail is also braided with ribbon. A wreath of dried flowers circles her neck. You can tell this unicorn is beloved! You stroke her mane and she turns her head toward you affectionately.

As you run your hands over the unicorn's silky coat, you think about what to do. There isn't any point in staying at the castle now that you know there's no silver unicorn here. Should you steal this unicorn and see if it will satisfy the warlock? Or should you leave the castle to continue your search for a silver unicorn?

If you decide to steal this unicorn, turn to page 109.

If you decide to leave and search for a silver unicorn, turn to page 118.

You've never climbed a metal tree before, and it is *not* easy! The silver bark is both freezing and slippery. You scramble up a few inches only to slide down again. You try jumping to grab the lowest bough, but it's too high.

Finally, you get the idea to use your shawl. You hold one end with your right hand, wrap your shawl behind the tree, and grasp the other end in your left hand. You lean back and slowly, gingerly, step your way up the trunk to the lowest branch.

As you straddle the bough, you feel victorious! You try breaking off a small branch, but it only bends a little; it doesn't snap off. Next you try a thinner twig. That bends more easily, but still remains attached to the tree. You're going to have to use all your strength. You brace your feet on the branch and grab the skinniest twig. You pull with all your might . . . and tumble off the tree!

As you crash into the ground, you hear a snap. There's a blinding flash of pain. To your horror, you can see a bit of bone sticking out of your leg.

Turn to page 100.

100

You shout for help until your voice is hoarse. When it's clear that only the silver birds can hear you, you know that you have to get home by yourself. You try standing, but immediately collapse, and your leg hurts worse than before. If you can't walk, you'll have to drag yourself home. You reach your arms forward into the snow and pull yourself a few inches. Each movement is excruciating, and your progress is very slow.

The sun sets and the wolves start to howl. You're too cold and exhausted to continue. You curl up in the snow and pull your shawl over your head.

That's how the sorceress finds you the next morning, but it's too late. Even she can't bring the dead back to life.

The End

Getting the vest out of the castle is surprisingly easy!

The next day, after you've taken the final stitch on the vest, you tell Nan, "I think this embroidery is perfect, but I'd like to examine it in full sunlight just to make sure. May I take the vest outdoors for a closer look?"

"That's a good idea!" Nan says. "Take your needle and some silver thread with you in case you need to fix anything."

As you carry the vest through the castle, everyone comes over to admire it. You have to admit it's your best work, and you hate the idea of giving it to the warlock. If you stayed here, you could embroider even more beautiful things. But then you remember that your village, and maybe even all of Flanders, is waiting for your help.

Once you're in the courtyard, you slip behind a wagon to change. You pull off your own tunic, and, shivering in the cold, put your arms through the vest. Then you shimmy your own tunic back over it. Of course, the vest is too big for you, so you have to tuck it up with your belt. You wrap your shawl tightly around you. You know you might look a little funny, but no one stops you as you walk past the walls and out into the world of winter.

You quickly find your hidden skates, and notice Wiets's skates are gone. You hope he's okay!

Turn to page 103.

As you glide along the river, away from the castle, you remember where the warlock was last seen. Your neighbors said he's been spending the winter in the ruins of a cottage not far from the windmill.

By the time you reach the mill, you're freezing. As you unstrap your skates, you remember the flasks of hot tea that were always available in the sewing room to warm the fingers of the seamstresses. Did you just leave the best job of your life?

You put that thought out of your mind and trudge past the mill to the ruins of a stone cottage. No one had lived there since the plague killed the last inhabitants more than a century ago, but the warlock moved in at the start of winter. As you stand at what seems to be the entrance, it occurs to you that the vest will appear more impressive if it's not under your tunic, draped over your winter-skinny body. You wriggle out of your tunic, slide your arms out of the vest, and adjust your own clothes again. You are just spreading the vest on the snow so you can fold it carefully when suddenly, the vest is yanked into the entrance.

Turn to the next page.

You blink with shock, not really understanding what happened. You poke your head inside. In the darkness, two red eyes glow. Surely, this is the warlock!

You are so nervous you can hardly breathe, never mind speak. The warlock makes a growling noise and you flinch.

You force yourself to inhale, then say, "I made that vest for you. It's covered with silver unicorns. Will you please end winter now?"

The red eyes slowly blink.

"This vest is of no use to me. I'm living in what is essentially a pile of rocks, so fashionable clothing is the least of my concerns. Here, you can take it back." He shoves the vest into your face.

You grab the precious vest. You're not sure what to do next. It occurs to you that you haven't been gone so long. There's probably time for you to skate back to the Duke's castle and tell Nan you were fixing some tiny stitches. You remember how much you liked working there, and besides, you still haven't learned if there's a silver unicorn in the stable.

On the other hand, should you give up so easily? Now that you've met the warlock, shouldn't you try to reason with him?

If you decide to hurry back to the Duke's castle, turn to page 112.

If you decide to try to talk the warlock into ending winter, turn to page 122.

You poke your head into the entrance and try calling the warlock again.

Taking a deep breath to summon your courage, you duck your head and step into the ruins. It's a mess! Over the years, stones have fallen and part of the roof has collapsed. You can see that the warlock has made a table of sorts by propping a plank on some of the larger rocks. There's a pile of fur where maybe he sleeps. You are just lifting one of the furs to look underneath when you hear a gasp behind you.

Quickly, you turn around to face a short, bearded man standing with his hands on his hips. His red eyes are blazing!

"What are you doing in here?" he growls.

You cower behind the table. You're too scared to answer.

The warlock grabs your shoulder and yanks you toward him. His eyes are only inches from yours, and you can smell rotten meat on his breath.

"Who are you?" he demands.

"Borah!" you shout. "Help me!"

"Oh?" says the warlock. "You're with my sister?" He grasps both your shoulders and pulls you even closer. You try not to look into his eyes, but somehow you can't avoid them. His eyes are locked on yours.

Soon all you see is glowing red. It seems like the whole universe is pulsing red. You blink a few times, and then red turns to black. You feel your heart slow and then stop.

The End

You know you have to have a look at the stable, so as soon as the vest is finished, you tell Nan, "Whew! I've got a blinding headache! Please, can I rest until I feel better?"

"Of course," she replies with sweet concern. "You've poured your heart into this magnificent work. Take the rest of the day off."

Instead of resting, you head to the stable. There you introduce yourself to Josef, the stable master.

"I've heard about your nimble fingers!" he says with a smile. "When the Duke gets home, he'll be delighted with the vest you've embroidered."

You can't believe word of your skills has even reached the stable!

"Tell me," you say, "does the Duke have a silver unicorn?"

"No," Josef replies, "and that's exactly what he's gone looking for. I'm sure you've heard how the warlock won't end winter until he receives a silver unicorn. The Duke is prepared to spend half his fortune to buy such a creature."

Before you can comment, you and Josef both turn to the sound of horses approaching. The riders are dressed in furs and one carries a flag.

Go on to the next page.

Josef drops to one knee and bows his head to one of the men. "Your Grace," he says. Is this the Duke? You quickly drop to one knee as well.

"Josef," says the most finely dressed of the riders, "I've had no luck at all finding a silver unicorn, but look, I did bring back a regular one." He gestures to a small unicorn tied to one of the horses. "Maybe we can figure out a way to make it appear silver."

"I have an idea!" you exclaim. The Duke notices you for the first time.

"And you are?" he asks.

"I'm the new needleworker."

"And one with amazing skills!" adds Josef.

Turn to the next page.

108

"There's lots of silver thread in the sewing room. I could crochet a silver jacket for the unicorn. It wouldn't be a real silver unicorn, but it might be enough to satisfy the warlock."

"We have nothing to lose," says the Duke. "Get to work."

You hurry back to the sewing room, breathless with excitement. You start crocheting a silver hood for the unicorn while other seamstresses work on silver leggings. Nan herself crochets the main jacket. It's your tiny stitching that connects all the pieces together.

Turn to page 116.

You decide that this is such a beautiful unicorn that surely it will satisfy the warlock. Even though you feel bad about taking it from the Duchess, saving Flanders from the endless winter is more important. The Duchess is certainly rich enough to buy another unicorn.

That night, you hide yourself behind some hay in the unicorn's stall. At least being so close to the unicorn keeps you warm.

When it's finally dark, you lead the unicorn out of the stable, past the sleeping guards, and past the castle walls. Almost immediately, you see that this is not a wild unicorn that's used to romping in snow. This unicorn trembles with every step in the snow. Ice makes her whinny with fear. She shivers in the cold night air.

Turn to the next page.

"It's okay, it's okay," you tell the unicorn, stroking her mane. *But will it be okay?* you wonder. *Will the warlock treat this unicorn as lovingly as the Duchess has?*

Have you made a terrible mistake?

You have to admit that stomping through snow in the darkness isn't easy for you either. Maybe it would be better to huddle together with the unicorn for the rest of the night and start moving again as soon as the sky lightens.

You settle the unicorn below the biggest oak tree you've ever seen in your life. *It must be a thousand years old*, you think. You drape your own shawl over the unicorn's back and wrap your arms around the shivering creature. Just when you think things can't get any worse, it starts to snow. Now you are really freezing!

You can't help it, but you start to cry. You hear the unicorn sniffle and realize she's crying too. Silvery tears roll down her nose and puddle at the base of the oak tree. Strangely, they don't freeze. In fact, the unicorn tears seem to melt the snow.

With each passing hour, you feel a little warmer, until you're finally able to sleep. In your dreams, you hear the unicorn sobbing.

Go on to the next page.

When you wake up, the sky is pink with sunrise. You blink your eyes. Where's the snow? You stand up and look around.

There are patches of snow here and there, but most of the ground is bare and muddy. You look up to the branches of the enormous oak tree and see leaves beginning to bud.

You remember Marie-Claire telling you about ancient oak trees with magical possibilities. Could this be one of them? Or was it the magic of unicorn tears that broke the warlock's spell of winter?

You wipe the unicorn's tears away and help her up. With any luck, you'll be able to get her back in her stall before the stable master notices she's gone. Then you need to hurry home and welcome spring.

The End

112

Without a word to the warlock, you fling the vest over your own clothing and trudge back to the riverbank. Your numb fingers struggle to strap on your skates. You take a deep breath, step onto the frozen river, and head back toward the Duke's castle.

You know you have no time to waste, so you skate as fast as you can. Surely Nan won't have missed you in just a couple of hours. When you reach the castle, you hide your skates. You take off the Duke's vest, fold it up, and hurry to the entrance. You greet the guards warmly, expecting to enter, but the guards grab you.

"The thief returns!" one exclaims.

"What are you talking about?" you ask.

"You stole the vest the Duchess had made for the Duke! And now you return, expecting your job back?" He shakes your shoulder roughly.

"I didn't steal anything! The vest is right here, under my arm." It's hard to move when they're holding you so tightly, but you push the bundle forward as best you can.

"You can tell Nan all about it!" says the guard haughtily.

Soon Nan is standing before you looking very angry. She pulls the vest out from under your arm and examines it.

Go on to the next page.

"I'm sorry," you cry, "but I just wanted to show it to someone!"

"Rather bad timing," says Nan. "The Duke returned and the Duchess was excited about giving him this, but no one could find you or the vest. I got in a lot of trouble because of you."

You hang your head. "I'm really sorry. I can apologize to the Duchess."

Turn to page 115.

Nan sighs. "What to do with you? You're the best needleworker I've ever met, but you can't be trusted."

"It won't happen again, I promise!"

To the guards, Nan says, "Take this one to the dungeon. She'll do her sewing down there from now on."

You spend the rest of your short life in a dungeon under the castle. Each morning a guard brings you finery to embroider, but stitching in the darkness strains your eyes. In just a year or two, you no longer see well enough to take tiny stitches, so you end up doing basic mending instead. A few years later, you're blind, and not long after that, the guards start forgetting to feed you. You die in darkness, hungry.

The End

116

When it's finished, you and the other seamstresses parade through the castle to the stable. You've never dressed a unicorn before, and it's not easy to slide hooves through the delicate silver leggings. When the silver garment finally covers the unicorn, you say, "Wait! One more thing!" You carefully wrap silver thread around the horn from top to bottom.

"This is excellent!" the Duke exclaims. "I'll take it to the warlock right now!"

You return to the sewing room, but the suspense makes it hard to focus on your stitches. Then you hear a *drip, drip, drip*.

"The snow is melting!" Nan exclaims. "I think the warlock is satisfied." Turning to you, she says, "Thanks to your clever thinking, we'll finally have spring! How lucky we are to have you here!"

Then it hits you—now that spring is starting, should you go back to your village? If you're going to skate home, there's no time to waste before the river thaws. On the other hand, working in the castle has been wonderful. It's warm and there's enough food. The work is easier than farming and a million times more fun, but then you remember Marie-Claire, Wiets, and everyone you love in the village.

If you decide to return to the village, turn to page 121.

If you choose to remain at the castle, turn to page 128.

As soon as you have a chance to leave the castle, you do!

While you are supposed to be carrying manure out of the stable, you put down the bucket and casually stroll through the courtyard and out the gate in the castle walls. Just outside, you see Simon the peddler adjusting the wares piled onto his horse-drawn sled. You go over to talk to him.

"Want a ride?" he asks you. "I'm heading to the silversmith in Bruges right now. With the money I made selling things to the Duke's family, I'm going to commission a silver statue of a unicorn."

"Do you think a silver statue will satisfy the warlock?" you ask skeptically.

"I'm going to find out! We have to try everything possible to end this winter," says Simon. "Come on! I'd welcome your company."

You feel a flutter of excitement. You've never been to Bruges before! Maybe you'll see a silver unicorn along the way!

"Thanks!" you tell Simon. "I'd love to join you!"

"I hope we can get there before dark," says Simon. "My horse is so much slower in the snow." He jiggles the reins and makes a clicking sound, but his horse doesn't quicken the pace.

You huddle under a blanket. At first, you're not worried at all. Simon is full of tales and gossip, so the time flies. He even shares a little bread. Because you haven't been outside your village in months, everything you pass seems interesting.

Turn to page 120.

120

However, as the hours pass, the sky darkens, and Simon stops chatting.

To keep your spirits up, you start singing, but only a few words have left your mouth when the horse neighs and abruptly stops. A man is holding its bridle! Two more men appear on each side of the sled. One yanks you off, flinging you into the snow.

Simon starts to argue with the men, but then you hear a punch, and he cries out in pain.

You try to fight back, but the robbers tie you and Simon together and roll you into a snowbank. Then they climb onto the sled and continue on. The fading sound of the hooves is the sound of doom.

Your heart is racing. You try to wriggle free, but the rope binds you tightly. Then you try screaming until your throat is raw.

"I'm sorry," says Simon. "This shouldn't have happened."

Days pass before anyone finds your snow-encrusted bodies.

The End

"Now that winter is ending, I really need to go home," you tell Nan and the seamstresses. The Duke insists on giving you a horse in appreciation of your work and clever idea. Everyone sadly waves goodbye.

When you reach your village, Wiets runs out to greet you. "Have you heard?" he asks. "The Duke tricked the warlock into ending winter!"

Would anyone believe it if you told them that dressing a regular unicorn in silver was your idea? You decide not to say anything. You're just happy that spring has arrived.

The End

"Why don't you come out and we can talk?" you suggest to the warlock. You certainly don't want to go inside!

"It's too cold to come out," he grumbles.

"*You're* the one who made it so cold!" you exclaim with exasperation. "You can end this winter! We all know you don't live here when it's warm! End winter, move out of these ruins, and you can have a beautiful unicorn-covered vest that everyone will see and admire."

"But I want a silver unicorn," he whines.

"You probably can't see in the darkness, but the vest has 108 silver unicorns embroidered over it. Come out!"

Go on to the next page.

"I want a *real* silver unicorn."

"Are you sure silver unicorns even exist? No one has found one," you say, but then remind yourself not to show how impatient you feel. You gently ask, "Why do you want a silver unicorn so badly?"

The warlock sighs. "I just wanted a special pet, and silver is so pretty. I like the way it shines."

"Does it have to be a unicorn? My friend Wiets has some very silvery cats. I'm sure he would give you one."

The warlock is silent.

"Would you like to at least see the silver cats? I could bring them here for you to look at."

The warlock snorts. "Okay."

Turn to the next page.

You're in such a hurry that you don't bother to conceal the Duke's vest. You throw it over your own clothing, put on your skates, and race back to the village.

Wiets is inside his cottage playing with his three cats. In the firelight, you have to admit that while they're a very lustrous gray, they aren't exactly silver. You quickly tell Wiets what's happened, and together you skate back to the warlock, each holding one cat. You've never skated with a cat in your arms before, and it definitely slows you down!

The sun is just beginning to set when you and Wiets reach the warlock's home.

"I've got silvery cats for you to see," you call into the ruins.

First a tattered hat, then a whiskered head, and finally the rest of the warlock emerges from the ruins. He's only a little taller than you, and you realize the vest would be too big for him.

You hold out a cat, hoping it won't be scared by him. "This is Rin."

The warlock reaches for the cat, and luckily, Rin doesn't put up a fight. In fact, the cat nuzzles the warlock's beard. He strokes her back and says, "She is a bit silvery . . ."

"This is her sister, Dottie," says Wiets as he offers the second cat to the warlock. "See the white dot on her forehead? That's how I can tell them apart."

Turn to page 126.

Dottie is just as friendly as Rin is. Dottie flicks her tail across his face and the warlock smiles. "They *are* very pretty," he says.

"Take them both!" says Wiets. You remember that his favorite cat, Shan, is still at home.

The warlock pushes the two cats through the entrance to the ruined cottage, then starts clapping his hands. At first you think he's just clapping because he's so happy to have the cats, but then you realize there's a weird rhythm that can't be random.

Suddenly, you feel too warm. You loosen your shawl and pull your hat off. *Am I getting a fever?* you wonder. Wiets yanks his hat off too.

The warlock stops clapping. "Enjoy the spring," he says as he slides back into his cottage.

You and Wiets look at each other in astonishment before bursting into laughter!

"Come on!" you say. "Let's skate home before the ice on the river melts."

The End

Your life at the castle is very comfortable. Now that you're known as the best needleworker, it's your responsibility to sew exclusively for the Duchess. You create exquisite dresses and embroider tiny silver unicorns on her shoes.

Every now and then, you return to your village to see your friends. While you're always happy to see them, you don't miss farming at all. You hurry back to the castle, grateful to take up the needle again. You've found your calling.

The End

You sigh and say, "I'll go look for the unicorn's parents first thing tomorrow."

"Do it now," Marie-Claire tells you, "while the scent of the young unicorn is still on you. In fact, rub your hands over this unicorn's body. If you smell like its child, you might attract the parents."

As much as you hate the idea of going right back to the snowy forest, you know Marie-Claire is probably right. Smelling like a young unicorn yourself, you return to the birch grove where you first heard the unicorn crying. You look around, then continue to the trap. You crouch down to touch the silver blood frozen in the snow and wonder how the injured unicorn is doing. Will it be awake when you get back? What will Marie-Claire feed it?

You are just straightening your legs to stand when something leaps onto your back and shoves your face into the snow. You hear a terrible snarl and feel teeth at the back of your neck. Your last thought is the realization that the scent of the young unicorn didn't attract its parents. It attracted a wolf!

The End

ABOUT THE ARTISTS

Illustrator: Suzanne Nugent is a freelance illustrator and a clay and paper puppet maker. She lives in Haddonfield, New Jersey, with her husband, two young daughters, a lop-eared rabbit, and a bearded dragon lizard, all of whom provide plenty of inspiration for her art. She has illustrated numerous *Choose Your Own Adventure®* books since 2004.

Cover Artist: Marco Cannella was born in Ascoli Piceno, Italy, on September 29, 1972. Marco started his career in art as a decorator and an illustrator when he was a college student. He became a full-time professional in 2001 when he received the flag-prize for the "Palio della Quintana" (one of the most important Italian historical games). Since then, he has worked as an illustrator at Studio Inventario in Bologna. He has also been a scenery designer for professional theater companies. He works for the production company ASP srl in Rome as a character designer and set designer on the preproduction of a CG feature film. In 2004 he moved to Bangalore, India, to serve as full-time art director on this project.

ABOUT THE AUTHOR

Deborah Lerme Goodman grew up in New York, where she saw *The Hunt of the Unicorn* tapestries that inspired a lifetime's fascination. Those amazing textiles also inspired her to study tapestry weaving in college! Aside from her three other *Unicorn* titles, she has written three other books in the original *Choose Your Own Adventure* series. She lives with her husband in Cambridge, Massachusetts.

For games, activities, and other fun stuff, or to write to Deborah Lerme Goodman, visit us online at CYOA.com

The History of Gamebooks

Although the *Choose Your Own Adventure*® series, first published in 1976, may be the best-known example of gamebooks, it was not the first.

In 1941, the legendary Argentine writer Jorge

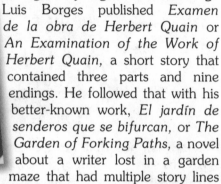

Luis Borges published *Examen de la obra de Herbert Quain* or *An Examination of the Work of Herbert Quain,* a short story that contained three parts and nine endings. He followed that with his better-known work, *El jardín de senderos que se bifurcan,* or *The Garden of Forking Paths,* a novel about a writer lost in a garden maze that had multiple story lines and endings.

Jorge Luis Borges

More than 20 years later, in 1964, another famous Argentine writer, Julio Cortázar, published a novel called *Rayuela* or *Hopscotch.* This book was composed of 155 "chapters" and the reader could make

Julio Cortázar

their way through a number of different "novels" depending on choices they made. At the same time, French author Raymond Queneau wrote an interactive story titled *Un conte à votre façon,* or *A Story As You Like It.*

Early in the 1970s, a popular series for children called *Trackers* was published in the UK that contained multiple choices and endings. In 1976,

Journey Under the Sea,
1ˢᵗ Edition

R. A. Montgomery wrote and published the first gamebook for young adults: *Journey Under the Sea* under the series name *The Adventures of You.* This was changed to *Choose Your Own Adventure* by Bantam Books when they published this and five others to launch the series in 1979. The success of CYOA spawned many imitators and the term gamebooks came into use to refer to any books that utilized the second person "you" to tell a story using multiple choices and endings.

Montgomery said in an interview in 2013: "This wasn't traditional literature. The *New York Times* children's book reviewer called *Choose Your Own Adventure* a literary movement. Indeed it was. The most important thing for me has always been to get kids reading. It's not the format, it's not even the writing. The reading happened because kids were in the driver's seat. They were the mountain climber, they were the doctor, they were the deep-sea explorer. They made choices, and so they read. There were people who expressed the feeling that nonlinear literature wasn't 'normal.' But interactive books have a long history, going back 70 years."

Young R. A. Montgomery

Choose Your Own Adventure Timeline

1977 – R. A. Montgomery writes *Journey Under the Sea* under the pen name Robert Mountain. It is published by Vermont Crossroads Press along with the title *Sugar Cane Island* under the series name *The Adventures of You*.

1979 – Montgomery brings his book series to New York where it is rejected by 14 publishers before being purchased by Bantam Books for the brand new children's division. The new series is renamed *Choose Your Own Adventure*.

1980 – *Space and Beyond* initial sales are slow until Bantam seeds libraries across the U.S. with 100,000 free copies.

1983 – CYOA sales reach ten million units of the first 14 titles.

1984 – For a six-week period, 9 spots of the top 15 books on the Waldenbooks Children's Bestsellers list belong to CYOA. *Choose* dominates the list throughout the 1980s.

1989 – Ten years after its original publication, over 150 CYOA titles have been published.

1990 – R. A. Montgomery publishes the *TRIO* series with Bantam, a six-book series that draws inspiration

from future worlds in CYOA titles *Escape* and *Beyond Escape*.

1992 – ABC TV adapts Shannon Gilligan's CYOA title *The Case of the Silk King* as a made-for-TV movie. It is set in Thailand and stars Pat Morita, Soleil Moon Frye, and Chad Allen.

1995 – A horror trend emerges in the children's book market, and Bantam launches *Choose Your Own Nightmare*, a series of shorter CYOA titles focused on creepy themes. The subseries is translated into several languages and converted to DVD and computer games.

1998 – Bantam licenses property from *Star Wars* to release *Choose Your Own Star Wars Adventures*. The 3-book series features traditional CYOA elements to place the reader in each of the existing *Star Wars* films and features holograms on the covers.

2003 – With the series virtually out of print, the copyright licenses and the *Choose Your Own Adventure* trademark revert to R. A. Montgomery. He forms Chooseco LLC with Shannon Gilligan.

2005 – *Choose Your Own Adventure* is re-launched into the education market, with all new art and covers. Texts have been updated to reflect changes to technology and discoveries in archaeology and science.

2006 – Chooseco LLC, operating out of a renovated farmhouse in Waitsfield, Vermont, publishes the series for the North American retail market, shipping 900,000 copies in its first six months.

2008 – Chooseco publishes *CYOA The Golden Path*, a three-volume epic for readers 10+, written by Anson Montgomery.

2008 – Poptropica and Chooseco partner to develop the first branded Poptropica island, "Nabooti Island," based on CYOA #4, *The Lost Jewels of Nabooti*.

2009 – *Choose Your Own Adventure* celebrates 30 years in print and releases two titles in partnership with WADA, the World Anti-Doping Agency, to emphasize fairness in sport.

2010 – Chooseco launches a new look for the classic books using special neon ink.

2013 – Chooseco launches eBooks on Kindle and in the iBookstore with trackable maps and other bonus features. The project is briefly hung up when Apple has to rewrite its terms and conditions for publishers to create space for this innovative eBook type.

2014 – Brazil and Korea license publishing rights to the series. 20 foreign publishers currently distribute the series worldwide.

2014 – Beloved series founder R. A. Montgomery dies at age 78. He finishes his final book in the *Choose Your Own Adventure* series only weeks before.

2018 – 2-Man Games releases the first-ever *Choose Your Own Adventure* board game, adapted from *House of Danger*. Record sales lead to the creation of a new game for 2019 based on *War with the Evil Power Master*.

2019 – Chooseco publishes a new subsets of *Choose Your Own Adventure* books based on real-life spies. The first two of the series are *Spies: Mata Hari and Spies: James Armistead Lafayette*, by debut authors Katherine Factor and Kyandreia Jones.

2020 – Chooseco publishes baby books adapted from the first 3 CYOA classics and they are so popular a full reprint is ordered two months ahead of publication.

2021 – Fall sees two ground-breaking longer, bigger books in the series, the side-splittingly funny *Time Travel Inn* by Bart King, and the evocative young adult fantasy novel *The Citadel of Whispers* by Kazim Ali.

THE WARLOCK
AND
THE UNICORN

This book is different from other books.

You and YOU ALONE are in charge of what happens in this story.

There are dangers, choices, adventures, and consequences. YOU must use all of your numerous talents and much of your enormous intelligence. The wrong decision could end in disaster—even death. But don't despair. At any time, YOU can go back and make another choice, alter the path of your story, and change its result.

Not long after you rescued your small Flemish village from a dangerous drought, the village is struck by another disaster: an evil warlock has cast a spell so that winter never ends. The only way he will reverse the unending snow and cold is if someone brings him a silver unicorn. The problem? No one has ever seen one. Do they even exist? You must decide: do you leave your village to battle the warlock on your own or do you go in search of a silver unicorn?